ON THE SHOULDERS OF GIANTS

by

**Arthur Ziffer &
Herbert Hauptman**

authorHOUSE®

AuthorHouse™
1663 Liberty Drive, Suite 200
Bloomington, IN 47403
www.authorhouse.com
Phone: 1-800-839-8640

First published by AuthorHouse   12/10/2008

ISBN: 978-1-4389-2954-5 (sc)

Library of Congress Control Number: 2008910183

Printed in the United States of America
Bloomington, Indiana

This book is printed on acid-free paper.

Characters

Isaac Newton

Catherine Barton, Newton's niece

Robert Hooke

Gottfried Leibniz

Clarissa Chaloner, wife of counterfeiter
William Chaloner

Scene 1

AT RISE: Isaac Newton is in his study, talking to the audience. He is holding a letter in his hand.

NEWTON

Oh, how I detest that scoundrel, Robert Hooke! Listen to his letter, which I received several days ago. (NEWTON reads the letter.) "Most esteemed colleague, Sir Isaac Newton: In order to explain the motion of the planets around the sun, I postulate the hypothesis that the sun exerts an attractive force on each planet, which, at each moment, varies inversely as the square of the distance between planet and sun and is always directed toward the sun.

I suggest that Kepler's three laws of planetary motion are nothing more than the mathematical consequence of my fundamental hypothesis; in particular that the orbit of each planet is an ellipse having the sun at one focus. Unfortunately, my mathematical talents (remember I am reading Hooke's letter) are not sufficiently developed to enable me to carry out this analysis. You, on the other hand, possessing mathematical powers unsurpassed by any living scientist, are superbly equipped to derive the laws of planetary motion stemming from my inverse square law. I respectfully suggest that you may wish to undertake this task, in this way, once and for all, explaining the puzzle of planetary motion in a most satisfactory way." (Letter ends, NEWTON continues.) Can you imagine the impertinence of this rascal, Hooke, presuming to suggest that I, the inventor of calculus, solve a problem, the consequence of which would bring glory and recognition only to himself, as if I were a mere technician doing the bidding of his master, who alone is capable of the profound insight required to formulate the theory needed to unravel this puzzling phenomenon? In addition, I find his humility disingenuous and his impertinence to be aggravated by the transparent falsity of his flattery, which I find patronizing, to say the least.

However, just between us, I must confess that the inverse square law has the ring of truth and I suspect might just explain the planetary motion in all its beautiful and intricate detail. In fact, having thought about this matter for some days now, I am quite convinced of its validity and, for this reason, am also certain that I would have arrived at the same conclusion myself completely independently. For this reason, I will pretend that I never received this letter and will not demean myself by responding. This, however, will in no way prevent me from deriving the mathematical consequences of the inverse square law in the expectation that planetary motion will thereby receive its definitive description in the, logically, most satisfying way.

The patronizing tone of Hooke's letter is particularly irritating, not only because he is a scientific mediocrity, condescending to offer guidance and advice to a superior, but because of the inappropriate relationship he has established with his niece, a mere girl twenty years his junior. I find his behavior in this respect despicable, especially since I myself have deliberately avoided time consuming romantic involvements so as not to detract from my scientific investigations. Hooke, on the other hand, spends so much time playing the philanderer that there's little time left for serious scientific activity, and his work suffers accordingly. I am convinced that the difference between Hooke's behavior and mine in this regard accounts in large measure for his meager scientific output, particularly when compared with the fundamental contributions which I have made. I can only hope that history will duly note the distinction between Hooke's behavior and mine. (NEWTON tears up the letter and stamps the shreds.)

You then may wonder why I have arranged for Hooke to come and visit me, which will occur shortly. I'm not sure why I am doing this. It is probably because of pressure being exerted on me from members of the English Scientific Royal Society, including the President, because of Hooke's position there as the Curator of Experiments. Well, Hooke may be able to twist arms of members of the Royal Society, but he has no power over me, and I will not give in an inch to him.

Scene 2

AT RISE: Hooke has come to see Newton.
They are alone.

NEWTON

Hooke, why have you come to my house? What do you want?

HOOKE

You know what I want, Isaac.

NEWTON

I want to hear it from your mouth.

HOOKE

I want my name in your magnum opus, the *Principia*, specifying that it was I who thought of the inverse square law first.

NEWTON

You did not think of it first. When I received your letter in which you discussed it, I had already thought of it. And, no, I can't prove this. It seemed rather obvious to me at the time; therefore, I did not feel it was necessary to publicize it.

HOOKE

You never responded to my letter.

NEWTON

No, I did not. I only respond when it is worth my while.

HOOKE

Had you responded, I might have been involved in what you have done in developing the Laws of Motions of the planets.

NEWTON

You were not necessary. I did it by myself.

HOOKE

Isaac, you have consigned me to be a secondary player in the game of science. I will only be known for that minor result of mine in Elasticity? Why, Isaac?

NEWTON

Because you didn't offer anything that I needed.

HOOKE

You don't think much of my work, do you?

NEWTON

You are not what I call competent.

HOOKE

May I ask why you think not?

NEWTON

I find your work mostly concerned with special cases. You don't look for general underlying principles.

HOOKE

We are all not as capable as you are, Isaac.

NEWTON

You mean that you don't work as hard as I do.

HOOKE

No, you have all those mathematical skills that I, and most other scientists, do not have. I, we, cannot compete with you.

NEWTON

Then go and acquire those so-called mathematical skills.

HOOKE

I cannot. Not only do I find mathematics too difficult, I find it uninteresting. I cannot learn it easily.

NEWTON

You mean you don't want to put in the effort. I never stop working. For me, work never ends.

HOOKE

I think that life should be more than just work. Where is the reward if one always works and never takes any time off to enjoy oneself?

NEWTON

Now you know, Robert, why you are a secondary player in the game of science.

HOOKE

Don't you ever take time off, Isaac? It is well-known that you drink your share of ale when you have finished working in the evening and want to unwind.

NEWTON

And it is well-known that your evenings are spent prowling the streets of London looking for women. A little medicinal drinking to help me sleep does not detract from my work.

HOOKE

There should be other things in life beside work, Isaac.

NEWTON

And, of course, you mean women.

HOOKE

Yes, I mean women. I have never been popular with women, Isaac. The few women that I have had were never ones that I really wanted but only those that were willing to go with me. I could never get a woman that I really desired. There was this actress once, who I used to go to see every night she performed. She was beautiful. Not only was her face lovely but she had this beautiful shape. During the performance, she would take off most of her clothes. She had this perfect figure. When she moved, it was a sinewy grace at its most magnificent, like a cat. Her legs were exquisite—long, curvaceous, narrow in the ankles, thicker through the calves, tapering again at the knees, and then thighs that were shapely all the way up. Even her feet were beautiful. And her torso—it was magnificent with beautiful curves everywhere. I used to wait backstage to see her when she would leave, always with some grandiose looking man, compared to whom I would be unnoticeable. One night she came out, and there was no one there to meet her. I went up to her and introduced myself. It seemed like she had never heard the name of Robert Hooke. I could see from her polite but disdainful look that to her I was no more than an unprepossessing, middle-aged man. Had I been the famous Isaac Newton, her look would have been that of a woman in the presence of eminence, and one very anxious to please.

NEWTON

I doubt that. Women don't know the names of scientists. But why are you talking about this? I hear the rumors—and if it gets to somebody like me it means that everybody else has heard it—that, at present, you are having a relationship with your niece, despite the fact that to some people that is incest.

HOOKE

It is not incest. Doesn't the law permit first cousins to marry?

NEWTON

But a niece is closer than a first cousin.

HOOKE

Isaac, you don't understand. I was failing when she came into my life. She brought me back to life. Actually, I had never been alive until she came along. She didn't bring me back to life. She made me come alive for the first time. She is the only woman whom I have ever been with whom I was also in love with.

NEWTON

Robert, one of the reasons that you are not one of my favorite people is because you care more about your relationships than your work.

HOOKE

I am sorry, Isaac, but this relationship is the high point of my life.

NEWTON

Robert, answer me the following question. If you could be the most famous scientist who ever lived but at the cost that this relationship had never happened, would you trade?

HOOKE

Why can't a man have both? Is that so much to ask for? Look at your mentor, Charles Montague, who is now Lord Halifax. He has everything. He is rich. He has been President of the Royal Society. Besides all that, he is very popular with the ladies as —forgive me for saying this — even your own niece can attest to.

NEWTON

Robert, will you never learn to control that filthy mouth of yours?

HOOKE

Isaac, it is common knowledge that your niece was involved with Lord Halifax and, furthermore, because of this liaison, he has helped you to get your position as Master of the Mint.

NEWTON

I find your presence here in my house, spewing out your verbal garbage, more and more distressing.

HOOKE

Isaac, is it possible that your hostility toward me has something to do with my having a relationship with my niece and you wanting to have one with yours but not being able to bring it about? Your niece and mine are very similar in many ways. They are both young, beautiful, well-disposed to their respective uncles, and, furthermore, we never saw them until they were grown and hence do not think of them as family.

NEWTON

I could never do with my niece what you do with yours.

HOOKE

But do you want to?

NEWTON

No, I do not want to. It would be unnatural.

HOOKE

Nothing that man does in unnatural. The pharaohs of Egypt used to marry their sisters.

NEWTON

That's disgusting; besides, women are of no concern to me.

HOOKE

No, don't you find your niece's presence here in your house a distinct blessing? Doesn't the room light up when she enters? Don't you find her conversation about the most mundane matters entrancing? Don't you hunger for her presence when she's been away for a while?

NEWTON

Yes, but that does not mean that I want to have a relationship with her like you have with your niece. How did your brother react when he found out about this liaison of yours with his daughter?

HOOKE

My brother died before the relationship started.

NEWTON

And if he were alive now, how would he react?

HOOKE

My brother was more concerned with gambling than with his daughter.

NEWTON

Then what does your brother's widow think? What does she say about your relationship with her daughter?

HOOKE

My brother left his wife and daughter in financial straits. I have helped them.

NEWTON

So you have bought your sister-in-law's acquiescence. How can you live with yourself?

HOOKE

And how will you live with yourself if that counterfeiter Chaloner is hanged? I know you have worked very hard as Master of the Mint to get evidence against him. Should a man be hanged for the crime of counterfeiting? At least nobody will die because of my misdoing. My niece has not been harmed. Also, I am beginning to see signs that she is getting tired of being shackled to an old man, and soon she will find a way to discard me. She will find herself a suitable husband who will take care of her and her mother, and I will have been just an interlude in her life. Have there been any interludes in your life?

NEWTON

And you, Hooke, will have to live with just being a minor player in the world of science with your publications that are full of words and more words and poorly written ones at that. But most importantly, they contain little mathematics or real science. I hope this is the last time you will ever come to my house, you reprobate.

Scene 3

AT RISE: Newton is talking to the audience.

NEWTON

Hooke made mention of the fact that I am now Master of the Mint. I have been very involved in solving the problems with counterfeiting that English currency has been having, especially with the practice of people taking gold coins, shaving off pieces of them, melting down the shavings, and from, say, twelve full-size coins making thirteen smaller ones. I have solved this problem by now requiring that all coins be milled on their edges; thus, with engravings on both sides, it becomes obvious when they are shaved. Hence there is no more coin shaving. My position as Master of the Mint gives me great power. For example, as Hooke said, I have finally gotten enough evidence against the man Chaloner, a wily counterfeiter if there ever was one, to get him hanged. I must admit that one of the reasons I am so angry with Chaloner is that he did make reference to my problems with women during his interrogation. The fool! Did he think I would forgive him that public humiliation of me?

But, of course, there have been others besides Chaloner who have brought up this issue. Hooke, as you all heard. But others, too. John Locke wanted me to meet some attractive widow. I got so mad at him for that that I wrote him a letter when he was ill wishing that he would die. I realize now that he thought he was just trying to do me a favor, so I have apologized to him. I don't know why I have avoided women. I need my time for my work. But, of course, to be honest, I have never trusted women. You might ask why. Well, one reason is because of my mother, although I must say I hate it when people complain about their mothers. Why can't mothers be human like everybody else? After all, a mother is just a woman, and, let's face it, women have a much harder time than men in this life. They have much more limited choices in how to live their lives, and this results in that their lives are very difficult for them if they don't have a husband.

My father died before I was born. When my mother remarried, her new husband refused to let me live with them, so I had to go live with my mother's parents. I must admit that when I was old enough to understand what had happened, I was furious. I even had a fantasy where the house that my mother and stepfather lived in burns down. God, how terrible it is to have those kinds of feelings. Anyway, after my stepfather died—he was elderly when my mother married him, although not so old that he couldn't produce three children—my mother brought me back to live with her. But it was too late. I have never trusted women, and that is probably another reason why I have avoided women. If my mother knew what I was going to accomplish, I wonder whether she would have left me to marry again. I like to think that she never would have abandoned me if she had known what I was going to do in the world of science.

Of course, there was one good thing to come out of my mother's second marriage, namely my dear sweet niece, Catherine, who now lives with me. This talk of Hooke about her relationship with Lord Halifax is nonsense. I trust my niece, and I'm sure she would not have had a relationship with Lord Halifax without being married to him. I must admit that I am annoyed that she is now engaged to John Conduitt. Why can't she just be happy living here with me? I give her everything she wants. I have done very well for myself at the Mint. Well, I guess the marriage will come to pass. At least she has agreed to live here with her husband after they are married, and so I will not lose her completely. But, of course, I will have to give her husband a job at the Mint, but that I can do. Finally, speaking of Lord Halifax, he did not get me my position at the Mint, as Hooke might have intimated. I deserved it and have proven to be very effective as Master.

But let us move on. The counterfeiter Chaloner has a wife, a very attractive woman I have been told. Despite the fact that he is a profligate, she wants me to spare his life. She has been so insistent on seeing me that I finally have agreed to see her. I know this will be unpleasant, but my niece, Catherine, has agreed to be present during the interview. I do this, of course, so that I have a witness in case Mrs. Chaloner wants to claim that I did anything wrong to her.

Scene 4

AT RISE: Newton is meeting with the wife of Chaloner in his study. Catherine Barton, his niece, is also present.

CHALONER'S WIFE

I have come to plead for my husband's life.

NEWTON

I am sorry, but he deserves to die.

CHALONER'S WIFE

But why? He has not killed anyone. Why should he have to die?

NEWTON

It is one of the possible punishments for his crimes.

CHALONER'S WIFE

You could have just as well sent him to prison, and he would eventually be free.

NEWTON

How can you come here and plead for your husband? He is a profligate and is forever committing adultery. Aren't you angry with him?

CHALONER'S WIFE

Yes, I am angry at the way he goes with every woman that comes his way, and there seem to be so many that are willing…There is something about that smile of his…But I don't want to see him hanged. He is all that I have, and he always comes back to me after his little flings. Please, Sir Isaac, let him live, even if he goes to prison.

NEWTON

No, he has been sentenced to die.

CHALONER'S WIFE

Sir Isaac, you have everything in life. I am told you are not only the most famous scientist in England but in the world. You are wealthy as well. And you are hale and hearty, still in your middle years. Why would you bother yourself with being Master of the Mint, wasting your time and energy on such mundane matters as counterfeiting, when you could still be doing your great scientific work?

NEWTON

Madame, for the wife of a criminal, you are very well spoken. May I ask how this came to be?

CHALONER'S WIFE

My father is a minister, and he made sure that I grew up with a reasonable education.

NEWTON

Then how did you come to marry a man like Chaloner?

CHALONER'S WIFE

I was like all the other willing women. All he had to do was give me that smile of his, and I was captivated.

NEWTON

But does being captivated translate into marrying him and going from the comfortable middle-class position of a minister's daughter to the wife of a ne'er-do-well, philandering counterfeiter?

CHALONER'S WIFE

There was also the problem I was having with my father at the time. He wanted me to marry some dull farmer who was very rich but who never learned to smile.

NEWTON

Do you regret having married Chaloner?

CHALONER'S WIFE

Sometimes, but it is too late for me to regret it. I am married to him.

CATHERINE

Uncle, what would be wrong in showing leniency with Chaloner?

NEWTON

Well, for one thing, I would be besieged with petitioners protesting the hanging of each counterfeiter.

CATHERINE

Uncle, certainly that cannot be the reason.

NEWTON

All right, since you press me, the truth of the matter is that your husband has made a fool out of us at the Mint for years with his clever tricks, and he does not deserve any leniency.

CHALONER'S WIFE

Please, Sir Isaac, I beg you.

NEWTON

No, stop this!

CHALONER'S WIFE

Please, Sir Isaac.

NEWTON

No, Madame, no. I won't. I can't.

CHALONER'S WIFE

Is there any chance that the severity of the punishment for my husband is because in some way you are envious of him?

NEWTON

Why would I be envious of a common criminal?

CHALONER'S WIFE

Is it possible that having been a great scientist has not been enough for you; that you resent the fact that my husband has lived a life so very different from yours?

NEWTON

What specifically are you getting at?

CHALONER'S WIFE

Could it be that you begrudge him the endless succession of women that he has had in his life?

CATHERINE

Madame, you are saying the wrong thing to my uncle.

CHALONER'S WIFE

Am I? I hear that the great Sir Isaac is afraid of women. Why could he not see me without you being here?

CATHERINE

I warn you to watch what you say to my uncle.

CHALONER'S WIFE

Not only will I not watch what I say, but I will go further. Sir Isaac, if you promise to release my husband, I will do anything for you. Yes, I say this even with your niece present. Are you shocked? What would be the harm in it? My husband would not care, and, even if he did, it would be my small revenge for all the times he played me false with other women.

NEWTON

I am not interested in anything that you could do for me.

CHALONER'S WIFE

I do not believe that. I see the way you look at me. You are staring at me. I have not been married so long that I have forgotten what that look means. Do not be hesitant and shy, Sir Isaac. There is more to life than books and your scientific theories. All your great discoveries will only benefit the world. Live for yourself, Sir Isaac.

NEWTON

I do live for myself, Madame. It is just in a different way than most people live. I am finding this conversation very unpleasant, and I wish to end it.

CHALONER'S WIFE

Sir Isaac, why are there no women in your life?

NEWTON

That is none of your business, you outspoken hussy!

CHALONER'S WIFE

Is there some reason why there are no women in your life? These stories about you and that Frenchman, Fatio—are they true? Is that what the great Isaac Newton is all about?

CATHERINE

Madame, how can you be so vicious?

CHALONER'S WIFE

Sir Isaac, you coward, stop avoiding looking into my eyes. Being a great scientist does not relieve you of the obligation of being a man.

CATHERINE

Madame, this behavior is unconscionable.

CHALONER'S WIFE

Don't try to squelch me, you spoiled brat. Would you not do the same for your husband if you were married? Could you say that you love a man and not be willing to do this to save his life?

CATHERINE

I would never marry a criminal.

CHALONER'S WIFE

Suppose he was not a criminal. Would you do it then? Sir Isaac, I hear that you are a very profound student of Scripture, as well as a great scientist. Tell your niece that no less a person than the biblical Sarah, the patriarch Abraham's wife, had relationships with other men to save Abraham's life, and, more, that she did it under the bidding of Abraham.

CATHERINE

I cannot believe that to be true, and even if it was, it is sacrilegious for you to identify your husband with the patriarch Abraham.

CHALONER'S WIFE

How dare you talk to me about sacrilege. Ask your uncle about sacrilege. (To Newton) My father told me much about you; that you are an anti-Trinitarian. He also told me that you had to have special dispensations in the oath-taking when you got your appointment at Cambridge. Do you think that I do not know why? How do you think the prelates of the Church of England would react if they knew that the great Sir Isaac Newton does not believe in the Holy Trinity of God: God, the Father; God, the Son; and God, the Holy Ghost? It was not so long ago that people in England were burned at the stake for your kind of religious beliefs.

NEWTON

Mrs. Chaloner, I am Master of the Mint. I have an army of agents to do my bidding. I do not think it is wise for you to threaten me. You are still young and attractive. You can find another man who will treat you better than your husband ever did.

CHALONER'S WIFE

Haven't you ever been in love, Sir Isaac? Don't you understand that I love my husband despite all his faults? Don't you understand what I am saying?…I know. You have never loved anyone or anything for that matter. You are dead inside, and it has made you cruel and heartless.

NEWTON

This meeting is at an end. (NEWTON gets up and exits.)

Scene 5

AT RISE: Newton is talking to the audience.

NEWTON

Chaloner's wife upset me more than Hooke did. She said that I have never loved anyone or anything. She is wrong. I have loved something. I have loved finding the divine order in the universe. It proves that God exists. If he didn't, would the universe be so orderly and harmonious? For those of you who do not know enough science to understand this, let me explain.

God set the planets in motion. But it was not a random motion. The Moon encircles the Earth once a month; the Earth goes around the Sun once a year. I set myself the goal of finding the secret of this regularity. Copernicus had recognized the fact that the Earth is not fixed but rather moves around the Sun. Kepler came up with his three laws of planetary motion. Galileo followed and refocused the scientific community on the Sun and not Earth as the center of our universe and brought up the notion of gravity, something which, curiously enough, I had thought of independently a long time ago as a result of something happening with an apple that would sound so outlandish that I will not mention it.

But then, to return to my explanation, I came along. It is very interesting, I think, that I was born the year Galileo died. He passed the mantle of Copernicus, Kepler, and himself on to me. I studied the work of these giants; men who could think the unthinkable. Just imagine the reaction of the world to these three men when they expressed the idea that the Earth was not the center of the universe. We all know of the troubles that Galileo had with the Inquisition and how he was forced to recant. What I have done is to climb up and stand on the shoulders of these giants and reach out further than any of them and further than any other man had ever reached. I reached, and I reached, and I reached.

Most men live their lives satisfying their own petty physical needs. I, on the other hand, have tried to rise above this and find some of the eternal truths that explain the regularity of the motions of the planets. These God-given eternal truths are, of course, the laws of motion. Some people think that science implies that God doesn't exist. That's nonsense. The laws of motion with their simplicity in explaining something so complicated prove unequivocally that God does exist and, furthermore, that he is a mathematician.

Of course, as some of you might already know, because of pressure from the Royal Society, to which I and Hooke both belonged, I had to put Hooke's name in the *Principia*, saying that he had discovered the inverse square law independently. Hooke never seemed to realize that the proof of the inverse square law was the important thing, not its enunciation. The proof is what the mathematician supplies. Mathematics explains the secrets of things. I guess that's why people don't like mathematicians—they can do something that nobody else can, and people resent that. Even Galileo, who was no mean mathematician himself, preferred Kepler to Copernicus, since Kepler came up with mathematical equations, while Copernicus just voiced the idea of the heliocentric universe. But, to return to Hooke, I never forgave him for his personal attacks on me. For the sake of revenge, I never went to the Royal Society meetings until after he died so as to avoid ever seeing him again.

You are all probably wondering how I would have treated the great Leibniz. It is easy to pay homage to one's predecessors after they have died. But what about the living? Are there any scientists and/or mathematicians who have been alive during my lifetime that I consider my equal? Halley, Wren, Huygens, the Bernoullis, Gregory, and Wallis are great, but they are not my equal. I am sure history will validate this opinion that I have no competitor. And what about Leibniz? He was more my equal than the rest, but I assert that he did not discover the differential calculus before me. He just published it first. I proved the results of the *Principia*, first using calculus, but, because I knew that very few people could understand such, I refrained from using this type of proof in it. I used mostly old-fashioned geometric proofs, which would be easier to follow. Furthermore, I always felt Leibniz was privy to some communications of mine to Huygens and others. To sum it up, I actually do not feel that Leibniz was such a bad person. It is his German disciples who have been so adamant in claiming his absolute priority in discovering calculus. I can say this because I once met and spoke to Leibniz, which no one realizes. This came about from a secret visit from him to me on one of his trips to England, which I shall now relate.

Scene 6

AT RISE: It is several days later. Leibniz has come to see Newton in Newton's study. They are alone.

LEIBNIZ

Hello, my name is Gottfried Leibniz. I am here to see Isaac Newton.

NEWTON

I am Isaac Newton. So you are Leibniz. What do you want from me?

LEIBNIZ

You never write to me, so, in order to communicate with you, I have to resort to a personal visit. I know that you have no desire to see me, so I will never tell anyone about this meeting if you wish.

NEWTON

Yes, I would like it to never be known that you and I came face to face.

LEIBNIZ

So it shall be, but may I stay and talk to you now?

NEWTON

You may stay since you have agreed to never say we met.

LEIBNIZ

Thank you, Isaac.

NEWTON

You are staring at me, Herr Leibniz.

LEIBNIZ

You are not as tall as I expected.

NEWTON

How tall did you expect me to be?

LEIBNIZ

Oh, about ten feet tall.

NEWTON

And you are not as tall as I suspected.

LEIBNIZ

What height did you expect me to be?

NEWTON

Oh, about nine feet tall.

LEIBNIZ

Touché, Isaac.

NEWTON

Herr Leibniz, I am surprised at how perfect your English is.

LEIBNIZ

Isaac, for many years, I have had to support myself by finding evidence that legitimizes the birth of bastard princelings whose wayward fathers happen to be rulers of small, German principalities. It has been necessary for me to learn to speak many of the languages in Europe in order to do my job. Knowing French and German made it easy for me to learn English, since English seems to be an amalgam of those two languages. But we have more important things to talk about.

NEWTON

Yes, we do.

LEIBNIZ

I presume we should discuss who should get credit for the development of the differential calculus.

NEWTON

Yes, and, with that as our goal, I would like to know if it is true that you visit Huygens when you go to Holland.

LEIBNIZ

Yes, I meet with Huygens every time I am in Holland.

NEWTON

Do you remember Huygens, open soul that he is, showing you a letter of mine that I wrote to him?

LEIBNIZ

Yes, I remember Huygens showing me a letter of yours.

NEWTON

Do you also remember that the letter had some discussion of calculus in it?

LEIBNIZ

Yes, I remember that there were some comments on calculus in the letter.

NEWTON

Do you feel that you got any benefit out of seeing what was in the letter?

LEIBNIZ

I don't know how much seeing what was there benefited me.

NEWTON

Could it be that you took advantage of me through Huygens?

LEIBNIZ

Haven't you done the same? Hooke has made it common knowledge that he wrote you about the inverse square law many years before you proved the laws of motion. Isaac, don't you agree that science is the accumulation of bright ideas, each scientist passing on his results formally or informally to others?

NEWTON

It is not the same thing, but I don't suppose you would understand that.

LEIBNIZ

Isaac, why can't we both receive credit? And remember, we are not the only ones involved in the creation of differential calculus. Do not forget the work of Fermat and also the work of your old mentor, Barrow. The only concession that I am willing to make is that you might have thought of it first, but I was the first to publish, and that might be the critical thing.

NEWTON

Thank you for at least that admission, Herr Leibniz. I did not expect you to admit that.

LEIBNIZ

You are welcome, Isaac, but I might not be so accommodating if we were not alone.

NEWTON

I see we will get nowhere with this conversation. Let us not discuss it anymore.

LEIBNIZ

All right, Isaac.

NEWTON

So we are finished with this meeting?

LEIBNIZ

Isaac, are you aware of how much alike we are?

NEWTON

Alike? What do you mean by that?

LEIBNIZ

Besides our interest in mathematics and science, we have another common interest.

NEWTON

And what is that, Herr Leibniz?

LEIBNIZ

Religion!

NEWTON

Yes, I am interested in religion.

LEIBNIZ

Interested? I hear that you are obsessed with it.

NEWTON

I admit to spending a lot of time and effort reading and writing about religion.

LEIBNIZ

The word is that you do not believe in the Trinity.

NEWTON

I thought that I had kept that secret.

LEIBNIZ

I have a great sympathy for that view. However, my main concern is ecumenicalism. I feel that the division of Christianity into Catholicism and Protestantism, with all the separate sects of the latter, weakens Christianity.

NEWTON

I see we both have the typical mathematician's desire for there to be unity in all things.

LEIBNIZ

Yes, unity gives power through simplicity.

NEWTON

That is my feeling exactly.

LEIBNIZ

Good. At least we are in agreement about something.

NEWTON

Well, is our meeting that never happened over?

LEIBNIZ

There is one thing I want to discuss before we end.

NEWTON

Yes, what is that?

LEIBNIZ

Chaloner!

NEWTON

Chaloner? Why would you want to discuss him?

LEIBNIZ

Sir Isaac, I want to know why you, the greatest scientist the world has ever known and possibly will ever know -- yes, I admit it; your work on the laws of motion and gravity will change the world like no other scientist's work before or after will -- can involve yourself in this execution of a petty criminal?

NEWTON

Chaloner is a willful man and has done things that I did not like.

LEIBNIZ

But whatever he has done, do you want your name, Isaac Newton, the man whose work, as I have said, will probably advance science more than the work of any other scientist, to be associated with such barbarism as the hanging of a minor criminal?

NEWTON

Would you say that if you were old, living from hand to mouth, and one day found that your life savings had been depreciated to nothing because of the currency crimes of Chaloner?

LEIBNIZ

That would make me angry, but is that justification for having someone hanged? Or is there some other reason for this hatred of Chaloner?

NEWTON

He has said things that have annoyed me very much.

LEIBNIZ

What things?

NEWTON

I can't talk about them.

LEIBNIZ

If there ever was a time to talk about it, it is now, Isaac. You are talking about it at a meeting that never occurred with a person you never met. And, above all, you are talking about it with a person who is very much like you.

NEWTON

I shall not talk about them; besides, I do not think that we are so much the same.

LEIBNIZ

I assure you the differences are only superficial.

NEWTON

I hear that you are quite the ladies' man at the various courts at which you spend your time. I seem to be the opposite.

LEIBNIZ

All my relationships with women are purely platonic. It never goes any further. Like you, I have this hunger for my work, which makes me hoard my time and energies; therefore, no woman has ever found a place in my life. Mathematics, as you well know, is a jealous mistress.

NEWTON

But you seem to be able to talk to women. For me, that is difficult.

LEIBNIZ

These conversations happen because I am at the court of my employer, and sometimes the court ladies pay some attention to me. Once even, I proposed to a woman, but she did not respond. Eventually, I lost my inclination and we drifted apart. But has not a woman ever caught your fancy, Isaac?

NEWTON

Yes, there have been several – one in particular, a Miss Storey.

LEIBNIZ

Can you tell me about her?

NEWTON

I knew her before I went to Cambridge. She lived on a farm nearby to my mother's. She liked me; I liked her.

LEIBNIZ

And?

NEWTON

I went to Cambridge. When I returned a few years later, to avoid the plague, which had finally reached Cambridge, she was married.

LEIBNIZ

That's it?

NEWTON

Yes, that is all I am going to say about it.

LEIBNIZ

Now you know why when you graduate college, you get a Bachelor's degree.

NEWTON

Very amusing, Herr Leibniz.

LEIBNIZ

I thought so.

NEWTON

I have a question to ask of you, Herr Leibniz. It is rather delicate.

LEIBNIZ

Oh?

NEWTON

It is about me and one of my old protégés, Fatio de Duillier. Do they say anything about Fatio and me in Europe?

LEIBNIZ

I have heard some rumors.

NEWTON

What kind of rumors?

LEIBNIZ

The usual garbage that the ignorant say about everyone who is superior to them in some way.

NEWTON

Tell me exactly!

LEIBNIZ

But Isaac, you cannot take seriously what guttersnipes say about you.

NEWTON

Tell me!

LEIBNIZ

All right, they say that your relationship with Fatio was more than that of savant and protégé.

NEWTON

Do you believe that?

LEIBNIZ

No, …but I did hear that you wanted him to come and live with you.

NEWTON

I invited him to come and live with me because I knew that he was having financial difficulties.

LEIBNIZ

But Fatio is a third-rate mathematician. He should be working in his father's store or on his father's farm, whatever his father does, or, at most, teaching in a secondary school. Why would you concern yourself with someone of so little promise?

NEWTON

There was something about him that intrigued me.

LEIBNIZ

Oh?

NEWTON

I have difficulty talking about this.

LEIBNIZ

I understand, but can you at least explain why, as I've heard, you broke off contact with him very abruptly?

NEWTON

I don't know. In the midst of the exchange of letters between Fatio and me, in which we were discussing the possibility of him coming to stay with me, I, all of a sudden, got very depressed. This depression alternated with bouts of excruciating anxiety. It was during this period that I broke off contact with him. I cannot explain the depression or the anxiety. This period lasted for over a year, and then the depression and the anxiety subsided.

LEIBNIZ

Was that the year of your depression that I hear about?

NEWTON

Yes.

LEIBNIZ

Isaac, it does not pay to dwell too much on the dark side of one's soul. There are things that are better not examined. Thank God that your depression has passed. But I must tell you that I also had a relationship with a younger man for a while. His name was Wilhelm Dillinger. We were very friendly for a while. But he wanted me to write a new will that left some of my fortune to him and when I said no, he abruptly ended our relationship.

NEWTON

Were there any rumors about you and him like there were about Fatio and me?

LEIBNIZ

Yes there were.

NEWTON

I guess we are more similar than I thought at first.

LEIBNIZ

I told you. But Isaac, it is now time for me to leave you.

NEWTON

You know, Gottfried, I have the feeling that we will never see each other again.

LEIBNIZ

I also have that same feeling, Isaac.

NEWTON

Well goodbye, Gottfried.

LEIBNIZ

Goodbye, Isaac.

(Curtain)